Adventures

with Ollie

The Ultra Embarrassing Moment

Carrie Pykett

ISBN 978-1-64140-433-4 (paperback)
ISBN 978-1-64140-434-1 (digital)

Christian Faith Publishing, Inc.
832 Park Avenue
Meadville, PA 16335
www.christianfaithpublishing.com

Printed in the United States of America

Acknowledgments

As a mother of two teenagers, I felt a calling to create something that would help all children understand that God loves them and will always be there for them. This book series would not have been possible without the hand of God. I am deeply humbled by and grateful for the opportunity to be His instrument.

I would like to dedicate this book to several guides on my and my family's spiritual journey. I had the honor to do service work with many Trinitarian Nuns (more formally known as Missionary Servants of the Most Blessed Trinity or MSBT). Sister Gail Lambert introduced me to several MSBT programs: the House of Hope in Massachusetts, Camp Trinita in Connecticut, and service trips in Alabama. Through these experiences, she and her sisters showed me the true joy of serving others. Sister Zelie, another Trinitarian nun, hosted our college's annual, two-week-long service trip. These annual service trips with her and my fellow undergraduate and, later, graduate school peers are forever imprinted on my heart. Initially, I thought I was helping others in need of many basic necessities, but quickly realized that I had much more to learn from them. Their faith filled them with a sense of peace and joy, even during the worst of circumstances. I would also like to express my deepest gratitude to Father Paul Soper, Father Michael Medas, and Father Tom McDonald for their tireless and joyful enthusiasm in sharing God's good words. My children, husband, and I are always in awe after sharing a conversation with them. They inspire my daughter and son's seeds of faith to continually grow and my husband's and mine to further deepen. You are a blessing to us and all who know you.

Although I have never met him, I feel God has given all of us a great gift in Pope Francis. May he continue to be a light for all of the world, and may we all embody his messages of love and mercy.

As always, I am grateful to God for my wonderful family who constantly inspire me with all the adventures we share: my husband Mark and our children, Hannah and Gregory; my parents, Ralph and Jane Fagner; my in-laws, Daniel and Deirdre Pykett; brother and sister-in-law, Joshua and Christina Fagner; sister-in-law and brother in-law, Allison and Joseph Donaldson; and Aunt Barbara Dekow. Then there are my cousins Patty, Justin, and Jason Dekow; Donna and Fred Dekow; and Stephanie, Fenton, and Brian Furrer. There are also all my nephews and one niece: Jake, Matt, and Nick Donaldson and Jack, Grace, and Tom Fagner. Although this book is a work of fiction, it is inspired by real life events.

Within the past two years, my children, Gregory and Hannah, and my nephew, Jack W. Fagner, tried new sports. As scary as these experiences may have seemed that very first day, all three of them showed real courage and faith. By the end of that first day or week, all three showed great promise in these activities and continue to do so. My nephew, Matthew Joseph Donaldson, inspired the naming of one of the characters in this book. Matt has always exhibited genuine kindness and care while mentoring his younger cousins and anyone who is blessed to know him.

This book series would not be possible without the continued support of Christian Fatih Publishing. Thank you for publishing books that spread God's love and His good words! I would specifically like to express my gratitude to my publication specialist, Cassy Byham, for her excellent efficiency and great humor and to the talented illustrators at Christian Faith Publishing's art department who, once again, did an outstanding job capturing the look and feel of the characters. I am deeply grateful for your continued support for and faith in this book series.

Finally, I would like to thank you, the reader, for getting to know Ollie, Kat, and Luke. I hope and pray that they will inspire you to embrace all life's adventures and to always walk in God's light and do His good works. Remember, nothing is ever too large or too small for God to handle. Give everything to Him, and you *will* experience the wonders he has in store for you.

Chapter 1

Fun in the Snow

"Give thanks to the Lord who is good, whose love endures forever!" -Psalms 107:1

O llie awoke to the sound of something lightly tapping at Luke's bedroom window. He slowly clambered out of his bed to investigate the cause. *What could it possibly be? A chipmunk trying to get inside?* thought Ollie as his heart raced faster at the mere idea. He placed his front paws on the low windowsill, moved the curtain aside with his nose, and saw a blanket of snow covering the ground. It looked so pretty and quiet outside. The first snowfall! *Wow, it sure is heavy if it is making that kind of noise,* pondered Ollie. *Ooh, and now I get to look extra adorable when my family dresses me up in my winter sweaters and jacket.* Ollie took a moment to envision himself in his warm and stylish jacket. He loved it when people commented on just how adorable he was when he wore these items on his daily walks. Ollie sighed deeply. *I do look so handsome in my fur-laced parka. Okay, it may not be real fur, but it looks and feels so cozy.*

Growing more excited about getting outside and being the first to mark his territory in the snow, Ollie worked his way toward Luke's bed. He had to make two attempts before he could fully make the jump up.

"Boy, I think I may need to cut back on my treats." Ollie laughed to himself. Once he caught his breath he thought, *Who am I kidding? I need my winter layers this time of year. If it were up to me, I would be able to eat even more cookies!* Ollie started to drool at this idea. *Now I definitely have to wake Luke up. I am hungry!* He gently walked onto Luke's chest and nuzzled Luke's chin with his nose. Nothing happened. Ollie tried it again. *What? Still nothing. I guess a dog has to do what a dog has to do,* he thought. He got closer to Luke's chin and gave him a big, wet wake-up lick. Luke wiped his face.

"Ollie, ugh! That sure is an extra wet one. What are you doing? Are you trying to wash my face?" asked a sleepy eyed Luke. While he yawned, Luke continued to rub Ollie's slobber off of his face. Ollie jumped down, ran toward the window and barked, "Come and see for yourself."

Luke slowly climbed out of bed and warned, "This better be good, Ollie." Ollie jumped up and down in front of the window. Luke pushed his curtains to the side and saw the very first snowfall of the

season. His face brightened with much joy. "Wow! I am so glad it finally came. I have really wanted to go sledding and ice skating. It looks like the right kind of snow for making snow people too!" Luke danced around his room and let out a loud, "Yippee! Thanks, pal! I wouldn't want to miss this!" He knelt down and gave Ollie a nice pet on the head then he quickly got back up and burst out of his room. Luke ran across the hall and tore open his sister's door. Ollie was right on his heels.

"Kat, wake up. You've got to see this!" shouted Luke. In one fell swoop, he opened Kat's shades. His sister barely lifted her head and mumbled, "What is going on? Is it already time to get up for school?" Rubbing her eyes, she tried to adjust to the brightness streaming into her room.

Luke shook his head. He went over and pulled down Kat's covers, reached for her arm, and tried to help her up as he answered, "No, but it's worth it."

"Maybe we can play outside before school," suggested Luke. Kat looked completely confused as she sleepily walked over to the window. Once she spotted the snow, an excited smile brightened her face. "Oh, it is so beautiful!" Kat let out a happy squeal and danced around her room. She stopped quickly and sadly added, "Too bad we didn't get more of it. I don't think it is enough to cancel school." Kat sighed deeply then happily shared, "Oh, but I do love the first snow fall! It makes everything look so clean and bright."

Ollie walked over to Kat, sat at her feet, and barked, "Hey, don't forget to thank me. I discovered this wonder today, not Luke!" Kat knelt down and looked at Ollie with such love. "Ollie, you are so adorable. Are you excited, too?" Ollie answered, "You bet!"

Kat picked him up and snuggled him. Ollie let out a happy whimper. Kat was a terrific snuggler. She would hold him close and give him lots and lots of little kisses. When she finished kissing him she asked, "Do you want to go out and play in the snow?"

Ollie barked a resounding, "Of course, but first things first. I have a very full bladder. Then I need to eat my breakfast!" Ollie's belly let out a loud rumble, and he ran to the doorway. Kat and Luke smiled at each other. Both of them understood what he needed.

They quickly followed Ollie down the stairs and practically collided into each other as they rounded the kitchen corner. Mom was already there, sipping her tea and reading the paper.

"Good morning, my angels. My, are we up nice and early," she commented with a happy smile on her face.

Luke was practically out of breath—partly due to his sprint to the kitchen and partly due to his excitement.

"Mom, can we *please* go out and play in the snow before school? I will even shovel the stairs," pleaded Luke.

Mom let out a little giggle then nodded in agreement. "Of course, you can. I have exciting news, though. You have a delayed opening, so you can play for a longer time and have a nice, big breakfast when Dad comes down. How's that for a plan!" exclaimed Mom.

Kat and Luke squealed with joy, gave Mom a big hug, then hauled themselves to the mud room at the speed of light.

"Hey, wait for me," barked Ollie. He sprinted to the mudroom. All the morning's excitement left him a little out of breath. He thought, *I already jumped up onto Luke's bed, then jumped in front of his window to show him the snow. I ran down to the kitchen and ran to the mudroom. I amaze myself. I did all this before breakfast.*

Kat walked over to Ollie's basket of items. She pulled out his favorite snow sweater. Ollie ran in a circle, chasing his tail. *This is what dogs do when they are excited. People sometimes just don't get this.* Ollie finally stopped. Now he was really out of breath. He took a few deep breaths then noticed that Kat was patiently waiting for him. *Lucky for me, she and Luke are the ones who pick out most of my clothes. They have great taste!* thought Ollie.

Kat sat down on the mud room floor and said, "Come here, you cutie pie. Let's get you all bundled up." Kat gave Ollie a nice rub down then put his sweater on with care. Next, Luke called Ollie over and fed him his favorite kibble.

Luke looked at Kat and explained, "This way, we won't have to run back in to feed Ollie, and you know he'll be finished before we even get all of our snow gear on." Luke laughed at his own thinking.

Kat looked up from tying the laces on her boot. She also giggled and expressed, "Great thinking, Lukey!"

Ollie shot his head up. *Okay, guilty as charged. I don't often take a leisurely meal. I am always so hungry. I just gobble it all up in a matter of seconds. Not minutes, but seconds. I know this is not considered good manners, but I cannot help myself. It is pretty embarrassing as this style of eating then leads me to increased incidences of gas. You know what I mean? In our family, Luke is known as the supernova. However, directly after meal time, I give him a run for his money—as they say. Luckily, I have figured out if I just sit near Luke during this time, our family blames him for the bad aroma and not me. Not a proud moment, I admit, but it keeps me looking good,* thought Ollie as he finished his last bite.

"Perfect timing, buddy," said Kat as she opened the door for Ollie. He followed Luke outside. He was so happy. The fresh smell of the snow and the quietness of it all made him feel peaceful. He also liked how it was much easier to track those rascally chipmunks that always teased him throughout the fall. Now, Ollie could not only smell their track, but he could see their tiny footprints. *In fact, I just spotted one by the grill,* thought Ollie as he ran over to that area and began his cat and mouse chase for the morning while Kat and Luke shoveled the stairs.

Ten minutes later, Kat and Luke finished shoveling the front and back stairs. Next, they began sledding down the small hill in the backyard. Ollie could hear them laughing a lot. As much as Ollie wanted to catch those chippies, he was torn. He also wanted to join Kat and Luke in their fun. He ultimately decided he could restart his chasing game later. He looked to where the chippies were hiding and barked, "You are off the hook for now. It's time for me to join in some sledding fun with Kat and Luke!"

Ollie trotted over to the top of the hill and waited until the kids climbed back up and joined him. Luke had pulled the sled all the way up. As soon as he finished balancing it at the top of the hill, Ollie jumped into the front position. Kat and Luke both laughed out loud. In a more serious tone Luke asked, "You gave up on the chippies?"

"Only temporarily. Don't worry. I reminded them whose yard this is," barked Ollie. He smiled up at Luke and added, "Now, let the real fun begin." Kat and Luke piled in behind him. They used their hands to push the sled forward. Before they knew it, they began sliding down the hill. Ollie just loved the feel of the wind in his fur! He joined Kat and Luke in their squeals of joy as the sled picked up speed. Ollie howled excitedly at the wind.

After the slide was over, Kat got up, placed the rope to the sled in her right hand, and started to pull the sled up the hill. Ollie thought, *I better hop into that quickly. Otherwise, I am going to have to walk up that entire hill.* Ollie grew very tired just from look-

ing at the hill. In a moment of panic, Ollie ran as fast as he could and luckily caught up with Kat. She stopped for a moment, and he quickly jumped into the sled. Kat looked at him and cracked up as he gave her his most adorable look. Ollie knew he needed to turn on the charm, so he had flopped his ears down and gave Kat his most earnest look. Kat giggled and said, "Okay, you can get a ride up the hill." Ollie happily barked, "Boy, this is the life!"

Luke gave Kat a forlorn look and tried out his impression of a cute puppy face. Then he hinted, "I wish someone would pull me up the hill." Kat laughed at him and said, "Me, too!" She looked at Luke again. He had moved his hands into prayer position, and just as he was about to plead with Kat, she quickly added, "Don't get any ideas. Ollie is heavy enough!"

Ollie gave Kat a shocked look as he pondered, *Hey, what are you insinuating?*

After about ten more runs, Kat and Luke's stomachs got the better of them. *All this sliding has made me hungry too,* thought Ollie. With Ollie quick on their heals, they headed back to the house. They wiped the snow off the sled with their gloves and placed it back into the garage. With chattering teeth, they ran to the side entrance of their home and entered through the mud room. A blast of warm air filled the mud room and greeted them. Ollie sniffed the air and grew excited as he recognized the delicious smell of bacon. *Oh, and I also detect something sweet,* he thought but couldn't quite put his paw on it. Mom called out from the kitchen and reminded the children to hang up all their wet gear in order to help it dry more quickly. The second Kat had finished helping Ollie out of his sweater, he took off for the kitchen.

As Ollie rounded the corner to the kitchen, he began to salivate. "Boy, oh boy, does it smell good!" he barked. Ollie grew more excited as he exclaimed, "Oh, that is definitely bacon! I just love bacon! I think I also smell cinnamon bread. Time for my next meal!" Ollie licked his lips.

Luke entered the kitchen and took a deep, long breath. "Wow, Mom! That smells *so* good. Did you make bacon?" he asked.

Mom smiled and walked over to Luke. She gave him a big hug and shared, "I sure did. With a delayed opening, we have more time for a leisurely breakfast. Plus, I am sure you are famished after all that shoveling and sledding."

Kat walked in at that same moment and shared, "I know I am. Boy, I wish we could do this every day." Luke nodded in agreement and said, "This *is* a great way to start the day." Ollie was sitting by their feet. He jumped up and down to show his support for the same thing then barked, "I agree. Let's do this every day."

This made Kat giggle, "I think Ollie wants the same thing."

Kat and Luke gave Mom a big hug. Next, they carefully washed their hands then went about setting the table with placemats, napkins, and silverware for each person. While doing this, they both shared their sledding adventures with Mom. Just as they finished, Dad entered the kitchen.

He made an exaggerated effort at sniffing the air. "Honey, did you make bacon?" he asked with a big smile on his face.

Dad was only allowed to eat bacon and anything with high cholesterol on rare occasions. If he could, he would eat bacon every day. So would Ollie.

Mom looked at Dad with a huge smile and replied, "I certainly did."

He walked over and gave Mom a big kiss. Luke made a pretend disgusted face and quickly and loudly exclaimed, "Dad, no public displays of affection!"

Luke really loved how affectionate his parents were but felt the need to tease them. When he did, it only made Dad more determined to share his expression of love for Mom, and this always resulted in his giving her even more kisses. When Luke was little, he used to work so hard to pop up in between his parents and disrupt their kisses. Back then, he used to tell Dad that he was going to marry Mom. They found that so adorable. Sure enough, Dad wrapped Mom in his arms, dipped her, and gave her an even bigger kiss. Just like the ones you see in the movies. Kat giggled. Luke protested again.

Ollie shook his head. Even though he already had his dog chow, he was still hungry. In fact, the smell of bacon was making him constantly drool. "Okay people, let's move on to more important matters. It is time to eat. Remember that bacon?" barked Ollie.

Mom giggled as Dad brought her up and out of the dip. She straightened her hair and suggested, "Let's sit and eat while everything is nice and hot." Ollie began to jump up and down. *I can't believe it. Mom is amazing. I swear she can sometimes read my mind,* sighed Ollie with gratitude in his heart.

Chapter 2

It Takes Courage to Try Something New

"I have the strength for everything through Him who empowers me." -Philippians 4:13

The family moved to the kitchen table and took their seats. As you may already know, Ollie loved to park himself directly under the kitchen table by Luke's feet. His reasoning for this was simple. Luke dropped the most amount of crumbs. Mom's friends always asked her if she cleaned her floors every day. She truly did not. It was Ollie's hard-working effort to always lick up every crumb like an ice rink Zamboni. This was what kept the floors looking fabulous. As Ollie liked to say, "It is a tough job, but somebody has to do it." Ollie grew excited as he watched something fall to the floor. "Yes! There's a piece of bacon. Keep them coming, Luke!"

Dad finished chewing his first bite of bacon. "Wow, this is so good. Thank you, honey, for making this great breakfast for us." With their mouths full of food, Kat, Luke, and Ollie happily shared their murmurs of agreement. Mom smiled at all of them and replied, "It is my joy!" Dad smiled back then took a sip of his juice before he asked, "So, did I hear the two of you shoveling the front *and* back stairs?" Kat and Luke smiled wide and exclaimed in unison, "Yes!" Dad finished his second bite of bacon and let out another happy sigh before he replied, "That is so thoughtful and very helpful. Thank you!" Luke finished chewing a large bite of food before he replied, "We were happy to help out, Dad."

Mom looked at Luke and asked, "Lukey, have you had a chance to talk to Dad about your winter sport idea?" Luke had just finished his soccer season and track and field did not start up until the spring. Last year, he played town basketball during the winter season. While it was fun, he didn't want to try out for the travel team as he and his family tried to ski on the weekends. Plus, they had a lot of winter family birthdays and celebrated them on the weekends. With basketball games every Saturday, the travel team's schedule just wouldn't work. So Luke had been investigating other options.

He took a deep breath then shared, "Dad, I had an idea yesterday at school. A couple of my friends are going to try joining the swim team this winter."

Dad finished chewing his last piece of bacon before he looked at Luke and asked, "I thought you wanted to play basketball?"

Luke took another deep breath. He didn't want to disappoint Dad. Just two weekends ago, he had taken Luke out to purchase a new pair of high-top sneakers for basketball, and he seemed really excited about the season. Luke had thought he wanted to play, but as the season grew closer, he knew he truly didn't want to. Luke looked at Mom, and she quietly mouthed, "It's okay. Go on."

Luke took one final deep breath then responded, "I did, but the schedule does not work out with our typical winter weekends. Plus, I really want to give my knees and legs a break from all the stress of stopping and running so much." He paused for a moment to see how Dad was responding. He was happy to find that Dad was really listening. With more confidence, Luke added, "Finally, I love swimming and many of my friends are joining the team. It is a walk-on team." Luke paused for another quick moment to catch his breath. "However, they are undefeated and have won the championship meets for the past ten years. I think it will be great cross training, and the coaches are supposed to be amazing," he finished in one breath.

Dad looked happily surprised. "That sounds exciting. When are practices?" he inquired.

Luke wiped his mouth with his napkin. "Well, I already ran this by Mom, and she is willing to make this happen if we all agree. Practices are at 6:00 a.m., Monday, Wednesday, and Friday. The season is a little over two months long," answered Luke.

"Luke, are you certain you will wake up early on those days?" asked Dad.

Luke nodded. "Absolutely! You know I am a morning person," he replied. "Plus, this will free up my afternoons for a change. It will give me more time to do homework."

Dad shook his head in agreement and stated, "That's true on both accounts. You are a morning person, and this schedule would allow you more time after school to finish all your homework." Dad started to nod his head in agreement.

Mom finished chewing a bite of food then shared, "Honey, I printed out the season's schedule, and it looks like they have meets every other week—a total of four, not including the championships." She took a sip of her tea before she added, "I think this will be a great experience for Luke. He has been with his other teams for so many years, it's nice for him to try something new and for him to work his body and his muscles in a different way. His pediatrician has always shared with us the importance of using all sorts of different muscle groups throughout childhood. Plus, this sport is great cross training."

Dad gave Luke a pat on the back. "I agree with Mom. Good for you, Luke. I think it is admirable for you to try new things," shared Dad.

Luke simultaneously smiled his happy and shy smile and said, "Thanks, Dad." He does this whenever anyone compliments him. All the girls in his family and at school think Luke looks adorable when he does this. Truly, it comes from his heart as he is a humble and kind person. Mom reached over and tousled his hair as she shared. "I am really proud of you, Luke. It is going to be a new challenge for you. I admire your bravado."

Dad took a bite of his cinnamon bread. When he swallowed, he said, "I can also help with getting you to and from practice some of those mornings or help get Kat to school." He thought for a moment before he added, "Now, you know you'll need to wear a speedo for practice."

Luke looked shocked and adamantly shook his head. "No way, Dad. Those are just for swim meets. The guys wouldn't be caught dead in those things during a practice. Remember, this is a walk-on team. I doubt we even have to wear them for a swim meet. I think the racing speedos are just for the older kids," Luke confidently explained.

Mom quietly observed the surprised look on Luke's face. "Monkey man, I think your Dad is right. I also think you are going to need goggles and a swim cap," she shared.

Luke laughed out loud then spoke with confidence, "Again, this is a walk-on team. I don't think they are that strict." Seeing the doubt in his parents' eyes, he added, "Plus, if I need those things, they'll let me know at the first practice."

Mom and Dad learned that sometimes, they had to let Luke and Kat find out answers for themselves. They decided to let Luke figure this one out.

Ollie got up on his hind legs, so all his family could see him. With their eyes on him, he barked, "Okay, now that this is settled, and it seems like Luke has a plan in place, we need to move on to eating

more breakfast. *Please*, more eating and less talking. I am so hungry. Remember, I chased the chippies, and I went sledding. Hello, I am down here. I need sustenance for whatever other adventures today might hold. Otherwise, I won't have any energy." Ollie pretended to faint, and he lay flat and completely still on the floor. This made his whole family laugh out loud.

Luke looked down at him and "accidentally" dropped him a piece of egg. Ollie popped right up. *What a guy,* he thought as he gobbled the egg up and gave his lips a nice, big lick. Next, Luke dropped him a piece of bacon. *Score!* Ollie sighed happily and thought, *This is the best start to a day.*

Chapter 3

The Ultra Embarrassing Cookie Tossing

"Let us not grow tired of doing good, for in due time we shall reap our harvest, if we do not give up." -Galatians 6:9

A week later, early in the morning, Ollie slowly lifted his head up from his cozy bed and saw that Luke was already dressed for swim practice. *Huh? It's still dark out!* thought Ollie as he covered his head with his paws and let out a frustrated sigh. Next, he tried to recover himself with his own blanket. He couldn't do it. Luke stretched and yawned. He saw Ollie struggling with his blanket and said with empathy, "I know, buddy. It is really early. You don't need to get up, though." He gently lifted up Ollie's paw print blanket and retucked him back in. Ollie, feeling all warm and cozy, instantly began

29

to snore. This totally cracked Luke up. He tried hard to stifle his laughter. He picked up his sports bag with his school clothes in it and glanced around his room to see if he had left anything behind. Seeing all was set, Luke quietly walked down to the kitchen. Upon entering, he saw Mom and Dad sitting at the table.

Luke loved watching his parents sip their tea and coffee while happily chatting away. He smiled at them and said, "Good morning, Mom and Dad." The kitchen was already warm, and the smell of waffles made Luke's stomach growl. He was hungry, but he also felt a few butterflies in his stomach. Luke was surprised that he was a little nervous about practice. He thought, *It's probably because I have never been on a swim team before. I just don't know what to expect.*

Mom smiled, walked over, and gave Luke a big hug. Then she said, "I made you a pineapple and banana smoothie last night, and here is one waffle, just enough to give you some energy for this morning's practice."

Luke smiled back, "Thanks, Mom." He joined his parents at the table and began to eat. "Boy, it is really dark out and very quiet this time of day," said Luke while chewing his waffle.

Dad gave Luke a big, teasing grin. "It sure is. Getting up at 5:00 a.m. is very different than 6:00 a.m." He chuckled.

Luke nodded in agreement and finished chewing another big bite of waffle before he answered, "I'll say. Even Ollie wanted nothing to do with this. I had to tuck him back in under his covers. As soon as I did, it seemed he was snoring within seconds." Mom and Dad both laughed at this. After Luke finished another bite, a thought occurred to him. He realized his parents were getting up extra early just to help him out. He looked up at them, and with love filling his heart he added, "Thanks for helping me get to swim team practice. I really do appreciate it."

Luke's thoughtfulness made both his parents smile. They replied in unison, "It is our joy!"

Mom then asked, "Are you excited?"

Luke thought about that for a moment before he answered, "Honestly, I have a mixture of feelings. Since this is new to me, I am a little nervous. However, I do love to swim, so I am also feeling excited. Plus, it will be fun to spend time with my friends."

Mom nodded her head in understanding and finished her sip of tea before she replied, "That makes a lot of sense. On a different note, I am so sad I can't drive you on your first day of practice. Somebody has to get Kat off to school. Plus, Dad is already going that way for work today." Luke looked at Mom and tried to reassure her as he said, "It's truly okay." He gave her a big smile.

Mom felt her heart melt. Luke was such a kind and understanding son. She always felt terrible when she had to miss any of her children's events. "Would you please call me right after practice and let me know how it went?" she asked.

Dad got up and cleared everyone's plates. "Of course he will," he replied. Next, Dad glanced at his watch. "Well, monkey man, it's almost time to leave.

Why don't you head on up and brush your teeth, then we should probably head out."

Luke rushed up the stairs to the bathroom, wet his hair, then brushed his teeth. Luckily, he had set everything up the night before in order to help make his early morning a little easier. He didn't want to change in front of the other boys, so Luke had thought to wear his beach swimsuit under his sweatpants. Last night, he also remembered to pack and place a towel and change of clothes into his sports bag. He quietly walked back downstairs to the mudroom and thought out loud, "I think I have everything." He threw his school bag over his shoulder then ran back to the kitchen and gave Mom a huge hug.

Mom took this moment and tried to hand Luke a pair of her swimming goggles. She suggested, "Honey, why don't you take these with you. Just in case . . ."

Luke emphatically shook his head *no* and answered, "Thanks, Mom, but these are so outdated. I think I'll be okay without them today."

Mom hugged him again and said, "I love you, monkey man."

Luke gave Mom another big squeeze back and replied, "I love you, too."

Fifteen minutes later, Luke and Dad arrived at the pool complex. Before Luke got out, they agreed to meet up at 7:10 a.m. just inside the entrance to the lobby. Dad turned and looked at his son and said, "Luke, have fun with this. Do your best, and as Mom always says, find the joy in it too."

Luke gave Dad a winning smile and replied, "I will, Dad." He jumped out of the car and with a quick wave, Luke rushed into the building. He easily found the pool changing room. He walked into the boy's area, found a locker, and took off his sweats. Luke swallowed hard as he quickly glanced around the room and realized he was the only one with board shorts on. The rest of the boys were all wearing long speedo bathing suits. Many also had bathing caps. To make matters worse, all the boys had a pair of goggles. Luke couldn't believe he didn't take up his mother's offer to use her goggles. *Ugh*, he thought. Luke quickly changed his attitude and rethought, *It's okay. I can do this.*

Luke caught up with his pals and headed to the pool area. Moments later, the coaches arrived. They called out and asked the team to meet up at the diving end of the pool. Once the team gathered there, they talked about what the season would look like.

"Gentleman, congratulations for making the choice to join this swim team. As many of you know, we have held the record for winning ten consecutive conference championships," shared the head coach.

The boys ignited with a loud round of applause.

The coach gently smiled at them. "There are two main reasons for this success. First off, was the effort put forth by each individual swimmer and, secondly, because of the team's shared faith. We coaches will challenge you to push yourselves beyond what you think is possible. Believe in yourself. Have faith. We also expect you to support and have faith in one another. We all have different talents and strengths. Make sure you share these gifts God has given you with your fellow teammates." The head coach paused for a quick moment before he asked, "Can I get an SGP shout out on three?" The boys all joined hands and on three they shouted, "SGP!"

The assistant coaches broke the boys down into heats based upon age. Next, with the head coach, they mixed the experience levels within each heat, so the newcomers would have the chance to learn from those with more skills. Luke was placed in a group with two friends, and with one kid he didn't know well and another boy who was well-known at school for his outstanding swim record.

The guy with the outstanding swim record went around and greeted each teammate in his group. When he got to Luke, he reached out his hand and said, "Welcome to the team. My name is Mathew." Luke shook his hand and introduced himself, "Hi, I'm Luke."

Mathew smiled kindly and cordially asked, "Have you ever been on a swim team before?"

Luke shook his head, "No, but I do love to swim." A friend of Luke's patted him on the back and turned toward Mathew as he shared, "Luke is a quick learner. He was our soccer team captain this past season. He is such a great athlete. He tried basketball for the first time last winter and was amazing."

Luke's shy smile appeared on his face, and he humbly said, "Thank you, I have been lucky to have great coaches."

Mathew nodded in understanding. "Awesome. Endurance and drive are two essential and great skills an athlete needs, and it sounds like you have them. Plus, we have the best coaches for this team." Then he looked toward the others and said, "Please let me know if I can help any of you with strokes, breathing, or anything else. I look forward to swimming with all of you guys. Welcome to the team!" Mathew reached up and gave each guy a high-five.

The head coach blew the whistle and instructed all the swimmers to make a straight line in their heat and for the first person to jump in when the next whistle blew. He further instructed that each time a whistle blew, the next swimmer in line was to jump in. For the warm-up, all team members would swim ten laps (twenty lengths of the pool).

Ten laps on the first day for a warm-up! thought Luke as his stomach did a little somersault. Luke was last in line and grateful for this as he would be able to watch his peers as they led the way. Soon enough, though, he found that he was up on the starting block. It was his turn. He felt awkward being up so high. He was only used to jumping into pools from the ground level. The starting blocks were almost as high as a diving board. Before Luke knew it, his coach blew the whistle, and Luke dove in. He gave his all for the first four laps then found he couldn't breathe well. He had already swallowed a lot of water each time he came to the surface. Luke, also, could not stay in a straight line because it was too difficult to see without goggles. The chlorine in the pool

was really high, and it was stinging his eyes. Never before had Luke thought of giving up on anything, but by the eighth lap, his arms and legs felt like they were on fire, and even worse, he felt like he was going to be sick. His stomach did another somersault. He quickly popped out of the pool and hurried over to the closest trash barrel.

Oh, no! This cannot happen! thought Luke. But boy, oh boy, did it. Luke sure enough got sick in the barrel and was miserable as he watched his pineapple smoothie and bits of waffle pass by his eyes. Luke had never done this before in public and felt deeply mortified. He took a deep breath and muttered, "Ugh! I can't believe this happened. It is only the first day." He was worried about what his coaches and teammates might think.

One of the assistant coaches walked over and gave Luke's back a gentle pat. Luke glanced up at him. With care and concern in his eyes, the coach said, "It happens to the best of us. No worries." He stayed with Luke until it seemed like he stopped getting sick. The coach kindly asked, "Are you feeling better now?"

With his head still over the barrel, Luke replied, "I am so sorry, Coach. I still do not feel well. Luke lifted his head up and asked, "Is it okay if I head to the locker room?"

The coach looked at Luke—this time with kindness and understanding—and replied, "Absolutely. If you continue to not feel well, just sit this practice out. If you feel somewhat better, join us for the dry land training. We do a lot of sit-ups, push-ups, and other core strengthening exercises."

Luke nodded and replied, "Thank you, Coach. I'll see how I feel."

Luke entered the changing room quickly. He wanted to cry. He felt so disappointed and embarrassed about what had occurred. Again, he thought, *I can't believe that just happened.* Still feeling sick, Luke decided to get dressed in his school clothes and call it a day. He sat on a locker room bench and tried to calm down his stomach. Once his stomach settled down, he placed his wet bathing suit and sweatpants into his gym bag then made his way to the lobby area. He waited on one of the lobby chairs and hoped his dad would show up early. After practice was over, his buddies saw him and walked over and asked if he felt better. Luke was grateful for their care. However, he still felt really embarrassed about what had happened.

"I am feeling a little better now, guys. Thanks for checking in," shared Luke. Out of his peripheral vision, he spied his dad coming around the corner and quickly excused himself. "I have to go. There's my dad. I'll see you guys at school."

Chapter 4

At Least You Didn't Clear Out the Pool

"God takes no delight in the strength of horses,
no pleasure in the runner's stride. Rather the
Lord takes pleasure in the devout, those who
await his faithful care." -Psalms 147:10–11

L uke met up with Dad at the front entrance, and he quickly led them out to the parking lot. Dad was a little surprised at Luke's silence, but thought he might be rushing to the car because he was super cold after being in the warm pool. After all, it was only thirty-four degrees out. As they entered the car, Dad ventured, "So, how was practice?"

Luke got into the car, buckled his seatbelt, and took a deep breath before he exclaimed, "Dad, it was a total disaster!" Luke hung his head low.

Dad looked at Luke and expected to see a teasing grin on his face. However, it seemed like Luke was serious. "No way. You are just kidding?" Dad gently ventured.

Luke shook his head. "No, Dad. I am not kidding. It was *so* hard." He picked his head up and added, "I was the only one without goggles, so I couldn't see. I kept swallowing water because I couldn't gauge where I was going. Also, I had on board shorts when everyone else had on long speedos, and to cap it all off, I threw up. All my breakfast passed before my very eyes," explained Luke with a deep, loud sigh.

Dad let out a long, low whistle and replied, "Wow, that does classify as a bad practice." He looked at Luke with love and concern and asked, "How do you feel now?"

Luke slid down the car chair a bit and replied, "Like a tire that lost all its air." Dad gave Luke a gentle pat on the back.

"That's understandable. You know, Luke, this stuff happens to many athletes, even the pros," counseled Dad. Luke gaffed at that.

"Well, it's never happened to me before. I think I made a *big* mistake. Maybe I shouldn't swim," confided Luke.

Dad grew quiet for a moment then gently suggested, "Let's see how you feel later on." Just then, Dad's cell phone rang. "Luke, it's probably Mom. Why don't you answer it," he stated.

Luke picked up Dad's phone and saw that it was Mom. He answered it and put her on speaker phone and said, "Hi, Mom. I just put you on speaker phone."

"Hi, honey. Hi, Lukey. Thank you for letting me know. How did practice go?" she asked.

Luke took a second deep breath since leaving the pool before he shared, "It was a disaster, Mom! I didn't like it one bit."

Mom was so surprised to hear this and gently asked, "What happened, Lukey?"

Luke cringed as he explained, "We started with a ten-lap warm-up. *That's twenty lengths!* I could barely finish eight laps. Then I had to get out of the pool because I felt nauseous. Mom, I barely made it to the barrel where I threw up all my breakfast. Pineapple smoothie and waffle chunks went everywhere!" groaned Luke.

"Oh, honey," Mom said with such empathy. "That's terrible. I truly thought you would have plenty of time to process your breakfast. I think we should just give you a small smoothie tomorrow and have you eat breakfast after practice."

Luke quickly responded, "Mom, I don't think I am going to go back tomorrow. Plus, I don't have the right swimsuit. Everyone was wearing the speedos like you and Dad thought. I don't think I can wear those. I was prepared to possibly wear them at a meet, but not at practice!"

Mom's voice was full of tenderness and understanding when she replied, "Sweetheart, I know you are not feeling great right now. Perhaps you have a little stomach bug. Your nerves or eating too much before practice can also make you feel nauseous." She paused for a moment to let that sink in. "How about this? You call me from school if you feel sick again, if you think it is a stomach bug. Okay?" suggested Mom.

"Okay," agreed Luke.

On the other end of the phone, Mom could hear how sad Luke was and suggested, "In the meantime, I will stop by the sports store and exchange your new high-top sneakers for a proper bathing suit. I can do this around lunchtime."

Luke let out a loud sigh. "I don't know if I am going back tomorrow. Mom, you shouldn't waste your time," he answered.

Mom paused before she suggested, "Well, I think it will be good to have it on hand. Plus, I know you. You are not a quitter. Let's talk more about this when you come home after school."

Luke thought about this for a moment. "Well, if you are going to the store anyway, would you please pick me up a pair of those cool looking goggles?" he asked. Mom felt a little reassured by Luke's request.

"Sure, but what makes them cool?" queried Mom. Luke's voice became a little animated.

"Electric colors like green or blue and getting the ones that have a reflection on the viewing part of the goggles, like sunglasses," answered Luke.

"Got it. I will do my best," she replied.

Dad interjected and said, "Well, we are here," as he pulled into the school's parking lot.

"Have a great day, my guys. Lukey, believe in yourself. It's okay to have had a bad experience. Don't let it define you or ruin your day. Dad and I are so proud of you for trying something new. I know it must be extra hard because you are used to excelling in your other sports. Keep in mind, you have been playing soccer and running track since preschool. Swimming, competitively, is new to you. Don't let this ruin your day," shared Mom. "Okay, monkey man?"

Dad turned to face Luke in the backseat and said, "Mom's right. We love you. Everything is going to be fine. Try to let it go and give it to God."

Luke honestly answered, "I will try. Thanks, Mom and Dad." Then he added, "Will you both pray for me?"

"Of course, we will. In fact, let's do so now," shared Mom. Everyone made the sign of the cross. They could hear Mom say, "In the name of the Father, the Son, and the Holy Spirit." Dad then went on to say, "Dear God, as you know, Luke is not feeling well right now. Please help him find the joy in today. We know you have a plan for all of us, even during our embarrassing and hard times. Please carry him and show him how to glorify you."

Everyone then said, "Amen," and made the sign of the cross again—kind of like hanging up the phone after a conversation ends.

Luke thanked Mom and Dad and told them that he loved them. They said together, "We love you, too!"

Luke hopped out of the car and gave Dad a quick wave. Dad then gave him the thumbs-up sign through the window. Luke smiled halfheartedly then entered the school by the side entrance. He worried his friends were going to tease him about what had happened at swim practice. Luke took a deep breath and headed for his locker. *Here goes*, he thought then silently prayed, "Dear God, please help me with this." Luke began to open his locker.

Mathew, the kid who excelled in swimming, came up from behind and gave Luke a tap on the back. "Hey, Luke. How are you feeling?"

Luke turned around and was touched to see genuine concern in Mathew's eyes. "Hi, Mathew. Thanks for asking. I feel somewhat better now, a little shaky, though. I hope it's not a stomach bug," replied Luke.

Mathew nodded his head and said, "That is the worst feeling." He took a moment before he continued on and confided, "If it's not a bug, I just wanted to let you know that you are in good company. Did you know that I threw up at my very first swim team practice two years ago?"

Luke looked Mathew in the eyes. "No way!" he exclaimed. Luke was truly surprised at this and somewhat comforted by it. Then he asked, "Did you really?"

Mathew nodded his head. "Yes, but I did it in the pool, and believe me, it wasn't pretty. I think everyone got out of that pool in record time," shared Mathew with a laugh.

Despite himself, Luke chuckled at the image then somberly said, "Boy, that must have been awful."

Mathew nodded. "At the time, it was. But it made me more determined to do well at the next practice," he said. Luke took it all in for a quick moment.

"Matthew, I really appreciate your sharing what happened." Luke paused for another quick moment before he added with awe in his voice, "Wow, I hadn't realized you have only been swimming for two years. You are amazing!"

Mathew looked Luke in the eyes and humbly replied, "Thank you. Truly, our coaches are the best. I just listen to them."

The bell rang and the crush of students entered the hallway. The surrounding noise was significantly elevated. Luke raised his voice and held out his hand, "Mathew, thank you for checking in with me and for sharing your story. I really appreciate it."

Mathew shook Luke's hand and yelled over the noise, "Anytime, teammate! I hope to see you tomorrow."

Mathew turned to head toward his class. The hallway, now full of kids rushing to their first class of the day, felt chaotic. Luke turned toward the opposite direction, made his way toward his class, and smiled for the first time since breakfast.

Chapter 5

Humble Pie Is Always the Right Gear

"As the heavens tower over the earth, so God's love towers over the faithful." -Psalms 103:11

O llie circled and barked, "Luke's bus is coming. Let me out, let me out!" Ollie began to jump up and down in front of Mom.

"I see, Mr. Oliver. Is it already that time of day?" asked Mom as she took a closer look at the time on her laptop. "Boy, today really flew by. Shall I let you out to meet Luke?"

Ollie jumped up and down again then barked, "Absolutely!" with his tail wagging a mile a minute.

Mom laughed and said, "Of course, you want to go out and greet him." Mom opened the door, and out rushed Ollie.

"I better high tail it. Otherwise, the bus will get to the stop before I do." Ollie began to sprint, then his energy waned quickly, and within moments, he was barely able to walk another step. "Boy, this was easier when I was younger. It feels like the driveway is growing longer each day. Plus, it is always harder to walk through snow," justified Ollie. The bus began to slow down just as Ollie finally made it to the stop. *I am so glad I made it. Luke had a bad morning. He needs me.* Ollie panted so hard he had to hang his tongue out of his mouth.

Luke climbed off the bus then waved to one of his pals. He turned around and spotted Ollie. "Hey there, boy. How are you?" Luke looked at him more closely then let out a little chuckle. "Wait, are you panting?" he asked with a huge grin on his face. "Boy, we need to have you run indoor track with Kat this season," he suggested with some laughter.

"What? Are you trying to break me? I am not a track star. Now, if there is a pie eating contest, count me in. That is my kind of race," barked Ollie. Ollie rolled over onto his back to emphasize his exhaustion. Luke laughed at that.

"You crack me up, Ollie! How about we head home and enjoy something more your speed? I wonder what kind of snack Mom has for us today," pondered Luke out loud.

Ollie quickly rolled over, stood up, and began to jump. "Count me in. I am always ready for a snack. Always!" barked Ollie. Motivated by snack time, Ollie picked up his pace to keep in time with Luke.

They entered the mud room, and Luke dropped all his school gear there. He washed his hands in the bathroom then looked for Mom. She was in the kitchen just finishing up a phone call. Mom held up her pointer finger. When she did this, she wanted to let the family know that she needed a second or so of quiet. Ollie sniffed the air to see if he could figure out what Mom made them for snack time. Sadly, Ollie picked up nothing. "How can this be?" He was worried that there would be no snack time. His stomach rumbled, and he sighed loudly, "Oh, woe is me! How I count on this time of day. I, also, exerted myself when I ran to Luke's bus stop." Ollie let out another huge and an even deeper sigh, then he crumpled into a pile on the floor. Mom finished her call and glanced at Ollie. Concern washed over her face.

"Is Ollie okay?" she asked.

Luke looked down at Ollie and started to laugh again. "He was fine a few minutes ago. I think he might be reading my mind. I guess we are both wondering what's for snack today?" responded Luke. Ollie lifted his head up, barked, and licked his lips.

That made Mom giggle. "My two boys. Between the two of you, there are six hollow legs in this house!" she exclaimed. Luke seemed to keep hitting these big growth spurts and along with them came long periods of constant hunger. Luke consistently felt like he could eat a house. Ollie loved this because it meant more snacks for Luke, and this translated to more crumbs being dropped on the floor. Ollie was always up for the job of keeping the floors clean and his belly full!

Luke gave Mom a big smile and said, "Guilty as charged."

Mom returned his smile then explained, "Well, I did not fix a snack for you because I wasn't sure how your stomach would be feeling. How are you, monkey?"

Luke was deeply touched by his mother's concern. He could see it written all over her face. "I feel better. I think it was a combination of nerves and eating breakfast too close to practice that led to my ultra-embarrassing cookie tossing," shared Luke. He cringed at the thought of it.

Mom walked over and wrapped Luke in her arms for a bear hug. "My poor guy. How awful for you," she said.

"How awful for Luke. He almost ruined my image of cookie time forever," howled Ollie as he covered his face with his paws.

Luke nodded and said, "It really was, Mom." Then, with more assurance, he added, "But I am okay now."

Mom saw that he truly was feeling better and gently suggested, "How about I pull together a snack for you, then we can sit and eat? And you can tell me all about it."

Ollie nodded and jumped up. "Okay, I am over the bad image. A snack sounds great to me!" he barked. This made Mom laugh again. His earnestness even made Luke chuckle.

As Mom moved around the kitchen, making a blueberry and banana smoothie, Luke shared more about what had happened at practice and his worry about what his peers and coaches might have thought. He paused for a few moments then added what Mathew had shared when they were back at school.

Mom walked over to the kitchen table and placed the smoothie in front of Luke. She had listened carefully to all he shared before she asked, "So, how do you feel about staying on the team now?"

Luke took a sip of his smoothie before he replied, "It's a really great team. The guys are super nice, and the coaches are amazing. I just don't want to let the team down. I am the absolute worst on the team. Honestly. That is not an exaggeration. I couldn't even finish the warm-up part of practice."

Mom took a seat across the table from Luke and said, "That is a good point. However, I think it is important to keep in mind that many of the other boys probably swam in the fall and maybe even practiced over the winter school break. Also, a good number of them have been swimming competitively for several years now. You cannot expect to be amazing right out of the gate."

Luke pondered this. "That is all true, but even so, I just don't think I can be an asset for the team," he shared with a heavy heart.

Mom took Luke's free hand and placed it between her two hands then gently stated, "Honey, you *can* do this. I know you. Ever since you were a baby, anything you've put your mind to, you have been able to accomplish. You always work so hard at something when it doesn't come easy. Then, one day, everything clicks, and you get it. Your coaches have, time and again, complimented you on your perseverance. Overall, you are a gifted athlete and, as such, have been able to pick most things up pretty quickly. I know that if you work hard, you will do well. Sure, in the end, you may not be the best on the team. God gives us all different gifts, you can't expect to have all the gifts." Mom smiled at him, let go of Luke's hands, then tousled his hair.

Luke began to nod in understanding. Mom continued on and reasoned, "Also, you made a commitment, Luke. I don't think it is a good idea for Dad and I to let you quit just because you had a bad day. You should never give up on yourself when things are tough. Plus, you truly haven't given this a fair try."

Luke nodded again and said, "I know you are right. I just don't know if I can do this."

Mom looked Luke directly in the eyes before she remarked, "Well, how about you change your perspective and expectations? Why not look at swimming as cross training for your other sports? You did share that you thought it would be amazing cross training for track and soccer, and I couldn't agree more."

Luke thought about this for a moment then replied, "This is true. I read that you use all your muscles when you swim. I also like how you told me it is easier on my joints."

Mom smiled at that. "That's the spirit, monkey! However, I would like to note that you are already a good swimmer. I think with the right training, you will do very well. If, for some reason, you do not, you will still be an asset to the team. Luke, you are great at motivating others. You have a natural God-given talent of picking up teammates when they feel down, and you have a gift of bringing people together," shared Mom.

Luke smiled shyly at his mother's compliment and thought, *She's right,* as he remembered how one of his best soccer teammates helped coach him and his teammates from the sideline. This particular boy had to sit out the entire season due to a preseason injury. Although this kid couldn't play for the team, he was the one who inspired them to do their best and kept their team spirit strong.

Mom reached over to the chair beside her and picked up a bag and said, "With this in mind, here you go." She passed Luke the bag. He opened it and excitedly glanced at all the contents. Then Luke looked up at her.

"These are perfect, Mom!" Luke exclaimed as he pulled out two speedo bathing suits and a pair of polarized goggles. "These are awesome!" He reached over and gave her a big hug.

Ollie shook his head in mock disgust. "Okay, okay. Enough with the snuggle time. I am still famished.

Remember, I ran my heart out to greet Luke. Now, I need sustenance, or I will faint," barked Ollie.

Mom looked down at Ollie and asked, "Oh! Is someone feeling left out? Did I forget your treat?" She paused for a moment to see Ollie's reaction. Ollie's ears were sticking straight up, and he tilted his head to the side as if he were saying, "Go on." Mom giggled at his adorable, inquisitive look and shared, "Well, it just so happens that there was something calling out your name at the mall, and I couldn't resist."

With a big chuckle, Mom picked up another bag and reached into it. Ollie's eyes widened as he watched her pull out *the biggest* bone he had ever seen. It was as large as Ollie's head and almost as long as half of Ollie's body. Luke laughed so hard then exclaimed, "Wow! Where did you ever find that, Mom?"

Mom joined Luke and laughed out loud too. It took her a few moments to collect herself before she answered, "It was in the pet store window—you know—the one we like to visit. The one that's just around the corner from the athletic store." Mom let out another burst of giggles before she added, "I saw it and had to get it. That *huge* bone had Ollie's name written all over it."

Ollie jumped up to take it and decided to high tail it to his favorite doggie bed by the family room window. It was so large he had to stop a couple of times to let his jaw rest. This made Luke and Mom laugh again. *Something this tasty deserves to be savored in the best spot in the house,* thought Ollie. He licked his lips with excited anticipation. He looked back at Luke and barked, "You'll be all right. I have faith that Mom can help you with today's problem." Feeling good about leaving Luke with Mom, Ollie raced off.

"Well, I guess we won't see him until dinnertime," remarked Luke with a huge grin on his face. Luke's expression quickly grew more serious. He said, "Hey, Mom. Thank you for getting me this gear, and most importantly, thank you for believing in me."

Mom gave Luke another hug and shared, "Dad and I always believe in you. As for tomorrow, give it to God. Let go and let God. Whatever happens, you will be fine. He has a plan for you. You just need to always place your trust in Him. No matter what happens."

Luke nodded in agreement, "I will, Mom." Luke grinned and added, "Now, may I please have a couple of those cookies you made yesterday?"

Mom felt a sense of relief. She knew if his appetite was good, Luke was truly feeling better. She smiled at him and said, "Of course, monkey man."

Chapter 6

Faith and Perseverance

"And I tell you, ask and you will receive;
seek and you will find; knock and the door
will be opened to you." -Luke 11:9

The alarm went off at 5:00 a.m. Mom tried to shake the grogginess off and slowly made her way to Luke's room. She gently rubbed his back and said, "It's time to wake up, Lukey." Luke stirred. Mom gave him several big kisses.

Hey, I want to be a part of that, thought Ollie. He felt a little bad about yesterday, how he had chosen his new bone over helping Luke. *I am going to send him off with joy in his heart today*, thought Ollie. *Even if getting up this early is super hard for me*. Ollie felt excited and happy about his decision. He took a few steps back then ran and jumped up onto the bed. Impressed with the result Ollie thought, *Hey, I made it on the first try again*. He shook his head.

Now, back to business." Ollie gave Luke some big, wet kisses.

"Okay, okay, I am getting up," said Luke. "Ollie, that is too much! It's like you're washing my face!" he sputtered.

Mom laughed, "He's just trying to help. I will have to keep this strategy in mind for the future." She turned toward Ollie and stated, "Good job, Ollie!" Mom reached over and gave him a nice pat on the head. Next, she turned toward Luke and said, "Honey, I am going to drive you to practice today. Why don't you get dressed, and I'll meet you downstairs."

Luke rubbed his eyes and groggily replied, "Sounds good, Mom."

Luke was a pretty organized kid. Once again, he had packed his school bag the night before, laid out his swim outfit and sweats, and he had already packed his school clothes and shoes inside his gym bag.

Ollie lifted his head up and thought, *What if I snuck into Luke's bag? I wonder what it would be like to attend classes with Luke. He is so lucky. He gets to learn new stuff all day long.*

Luke quickly got dressed. Ollie yawned then thought, *Nah, it's too early for me. Plus, Luke is gone for a really long time. I will need more sleep after Luke heads off to school.* Ollie yawned, and thought, *It would be so nice to just jump in bed with Kat. All cozy under the blankets. I really could fall back to sleep.* Ollie was tempted to run into Kat's room and make this idea a reality. However, his love for Luke won him over. *I have to do the right thing. Luke needs me now. I need to be there for him.*

Luke grabbed his bag, raced down the stairs, and rounded the corner to the kitchen. Ollie slowly and reluctantly followed him. Mom had her jacket on, a small to-go cup in her right hand, and her purse in the other when she asked, "Are you ready to go?"

Luke nodded his head. "I am." Ollie had his leash in his mouth and tried to bark, "I am ready, too."

This made both Mom and Luke chuckle.

Luke took a long, deep breath. He grabbed his winter jacket, and as he was putting it on, he confided, "Mom, will you please say a prayer for me? I am a little nervous."

Mom stopped lacing up her boots and reached for Luke's hand. "Absolutely. In fact, let's say one now, together," she suggested.

Ollie got up on his hind legs and placed them on Luke's left calf.

Mom and Luke made the sign of the cross, then they both clasped their hands together. Mom prayed, "Dear God, please help Luke today, no matter what happens. As you know, he is nervous. Please take this from him and guide him. We hope and pray that all of our family will do your good works today, that we will all glorify you. We also pray for all those in need. Amen." Mom and Luke made the sign of the cross again then headed for the car.

Ollie trotted beside Luke with his leash still in his mouth. Luke got into the backseat and buckled himself in. Ollie sat directly on his lap. Mom started up the car then turned the radio to Luke's favorite country music station. He and Mom sang along to their usual top choices. Ollie howled along. This kept making Luke crack up with laughter.

Before they knew it, they had arrived at the sports complex. The pool was only fifteen minutes away, so it truly felt to Luke like he blinked his eyes then they had arrived. Before getting out of the car, Luke gave Ollie one big pet on the head then gave Mom a big hug. She smiled at him and reminded, "I will see you after practice. Listen, remember to give any worry to God. Go in there, do your best, and find the joy in it."

Ollie barked, "You've got this Luke. Just have fun. Let go and let God."

"I will. Thank you both," answered Luke.

Luke raced into the building. It sure was cold out at 6:00 a.m. The locker room, however, felt like a sauna in comparison. This made it easier for Luke and the other guys to change out of their sweats and just wear their bathing suits. Mathew joined up with Luke and gave him a joy-filled smile.

"Hey, I am sure glad to see you," Mathew said. "I knew you weren't a quitter. I have a good feeling about you, my friend." He raised his hand for a high-five.

"Thanks for the vote of confidence," replied Luke as he returned Mathew's high five.

The guys headed out to the pool area. Today, the coaches had the team start with dry land training. Luke was so used to doing these exercises with his other teams that he outshone the rest of the group. This helped to build up his confidence a little more.

Next, the coaches broke the boys down into the same heats they were in on the first day of practice.

Luke was relieved to be with the same guys. He thought, *After all, they've already seen me toss my cookies. What could be worse?* When Luke's turn came to dive into the pool, he took a deep breath and he silently said a quick prayer, *Dear God, please help me to do my best. Whatever happens, let me trust in your ways.* Luke felt a strong sense of peace wash over him. He knew he was in God's hands. Without any feelings of worry, he jumped into the pool filled with hope and enthusiasm.

Luke finished all ten laps with no problem. He did not experience any feeling of nausea, and he did not swallow any pool water. Just as surprisingly, he was able to keep up with the guys in his leg. When Luke had finally completed his last twenty-five meters, he took a moment to take in what happened. Feelings of peace and joy washed over him. He said a silent prayer, *Thank you, God. Thank you so much for your help.* With a heart overflowing with happiness and gratitude, he started to get out of the pool. As soon as Luke landed on the pool decking, he was blasted with cheers from the peers in his heat. In fact, one of his teammates teased, "Wow! Are you really the same guy from yesterday?"

Luke laughed at that and honestly answered, "It's me."

One of the guys asked with awe in his tone, "What is your secret? I need to get me some of that."

Luke honestly shared, "I said a quick prayer before practice."

Several of the teammates shared that they also prayed before swim meets, tests, and for help with everyday things.

Matthew chimed in, "God is good."

Another teammate added, "All the time! Plus, I think having the proper goggles kept you from swallowing so much water and totally zigzagging all around the pool."

Luke looked at the boy and saw that he was kindly teasing him. Luke laughed and added, "That and I also avoided eating breakfast before practice. I decided it might be best to wait and eat afterward."

His teammates chuckled and nodded in agreement. One of the other boys added, "Thank you! We didn't want to see any food chunks floating around in the pool." Luke burst out laughing at that.

Mathew patted Luke on the back then exclaimed, "That was fantastic! If this is the improvement you made in just one day, I truly look forward to seeing what you'll accomplish after a full season with the team!" The other teammates cheered at this sentiment. The head coach, followed by the assistant coach, joined the boys. He shared, "Son, that was an amazing difference from yesterday. I am going to keep my eye on you. I think we might be able to expect great things from you." The team cheered, again, for Luke.

Luke's heart was filled with such gratitude. He realized how happy he was that his family had encouraged him to stay on the team. Although he had heard this many times, he truly realized that he was never alone. No matter the obstacle. The big guy was always there. He would always have Luke's back. He said another silent prayer, *Thank you, God! Thank you for the gift of my family, and thank you for always being there for me. I could not have done this adventure without you!*

The End

About the Author

Carrie Pykett, the mother of two teenagers, felt a calling to create something that would help children understand that God loves them and that He is always there for them. Her faith, professional training, life experiences, master's degree in psychology, and extensive work with youth and children led to the creation of this book and the other books in this series.

Professionally, Carrie worked in higher education for seven years and later was the founding executive director of then Steppingstones, now the Krempels Center (postrehabilitation center for people living with stroke, tumor, and traumatic brain injury). As a passionate educator and volunteer, she has taken young adults and youth on several outreach trips to help serve those in dire need (from building homes in the United States to coordinating outreach trips to help those in immediate need of food, clothing, and shelter after a natural disaster). She has taught CCD at her local church for over ten years (grades two to ten) and has been an active Eucharistic minister since 1992 (serving at her college church, a hospital, and at her local church).

Today's contemporary way of living, the onset of puberty, and the navigation of other normal developmental stages are often confusing and overwhelming for many children. Carrie carefully designed this book series to show children—ages eight to twelve and, sometimes, ten to fourteen—how to pray, why to lean on God, and how His way is the way to celebrate and embrace all life's adventures. *Adventures with Ollie: the Ultra Embarrassing Moment* is her third book in the series. Future topics include helping a friend in need, the new kid, social media and cyberbullying, friendship turned sour, never letting a seed of hatred grow, and the death of a loved one. Her first two books focus on jealousy (*Adventures with Ollie: Beware of the Green Monster*) and the importance of focusing on the ability versus the disability in oneself and others (*Adventures with Ollie: See the Ability*).

Carrie lives in Massachusetts with her loving family and writes from Massachusetts and Maine. She is grateful for the adventures God provides for her to share with her husband, two teenagers, and their two dogs.

CPSIA information can be obtained
at www.ICGtesting.com
Printed in the USA
BVHW072256171218
535790BV00012B/1139/P